Rapunzel

STERLING CHILDREN'S BOOKS
New York

TEXT ADAPTATION GIADA FRANCIA • GRAPHIC DESIGN MARINELLA DEBERNARDI

FROM A FAIRY TALE BY THE
Brothers Grimm

ILLUSTRATIONS BY
Francesca Rossi

In a small village nestled among the hills, there lived a man and his wife. The man, Nicholas, had always been a very nervous fellow. His wife, Anna, on the other hand, was completely different. While he was thoughtful and serious, she was a lively women who loved to laugh and joke. Yet against all the odds, they loved each other greatly. And as it so happened, they were expecting a baby.

During this time, Nicholas worked at the market all day while Anna stayed at home. Their home was a humble cottage, which sat next to a large house with a magnificent garden. In the village, people whispered that the old woman who lived there was a witch.

One beautiful spring morning, Anna looked out the window and sighed. She didn't want to stay at home on such a nice day, so she decided to visit her husband at the market. As she left the cottage, she walked past the large stone wall that guarded their elderly neighbor's house. When she reached the end of the wall, she peeked around the edge to admire the garden.

The garden of the house next door was full of blooming flowers and lush, ripe vegetables. It was rumored that the old woman grew magical plants to make spells and potions. What was certain, Anna thought, was that they looked delicious.

"If only I had a garden like our neighbor's," she said to herself. "I could cook all those wonderful vegetables."

Among the rows of vegetables, she spotted a patch of a salad plant called rapunzel. As she gazed at the rapunzel, she felt a growing urge to eat some. Overcome by her desire, she rushed to the market to find Nicholas.

When she finally reached Nicholas, he was surprised to see her. Noticing that she had rushed and was out of breath, his surprise quickly turned to concern.

"What is the matter, my darling? Has something happened at home? Is it serious?"

"It's very serious," she joked. "I'm hungry!"

Nicholas laughed, then became worried again. "Please, don't run! You might fall! With the baby on the way, you have to look after yourself."

"But looking after myself means being all alone in the cottage. It is so boring," she replied unhappily.

"My dear, I'm not asking much. This child is a gift from heaven and I don't want anything to happen." Nicholas kissed her. "Now go home and I'll see you tonight. What do you want for dinner? I'll bring anything you want."

"I would like some rapunzel!"

"Where will I find that?"

"In our neighbor's garden."

"You want me to sneak into the garden of that witch? But if she catches me . . ."

"You said I could have anything! Just don't get caught."

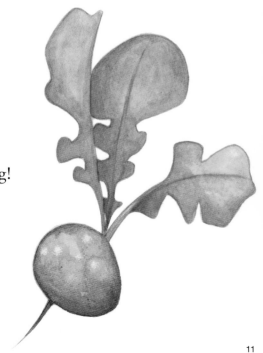

When darkness fell, Nicholas approached the high wall that surrounded the garden. He was very scared. Although he had never seen her come out of the house, people said terrible things about the old lady who lived there. He had heard that anyone who dared to knock on her door was never seen again!

Carefully, he crept into the vegetable garden. After collecting a handful of rapunzel, he hurried home and shut the door behind him with great relief.

"I've done it!" he cried. "But I'm telling you, I'm never going back into that garden."

That night, Anna prepared a delicious meal of rapunzel. And perhaps the plant really was bewitched; after tasting its delicious leaves, she refused to eat anything else. She didn't eat for days and quickly became ill.

Nicholas was desperate, so he decided to sneak back into the neighbor's garden. This time, however, he was not so lucky. When he turned around to go home with his arms full of vegetables, he ran into the old woman. Nicholas shook with fear.

"You're stealing my vegetables!" the old woman shrieked. "Do you know what I do to thieves?"

"I'm sorry! They're for my wife. She's expecting a baby and can't eat anything else. She fell ill and I'm worried about her!" stammered Nicholas.

The witch pointed a bony finger at him. "I will let you go, but only if you give me your firstborn child."

Nicholas was too afraid to say no. He promised the witch his firstborn, then quickly fled.

On returning home he told Anna what had happened. But she dismissed it with a smile. "She was joking! She wanted to scare you and you fell for it."

Nicholas thought she must be right, and they soon forgot about the witch. Shortly after, their beautiful baby girl was born and they were filled with joy.

After a few years, however, the witch knocked on their door. "You promised me your firstborn. I've come to collect her."

Nicholas and Anna tried to hide the little girl, but the witch burst into the cottage and took her.

The witch named the child Rapunzel and took her far, far away. Together they lived in a small house hidden deep in the forest. Few people ever visited those parts, but when they did, the witch told everyone she was the child's grandmother. She let them believe that the girl had been orphaned in a tragic accident. The witch told the same story to Rapunzel, who never doubted her words.

After years in the forest, the witch became very fond of the girl. She showed her the kindness and love of a real grandmother. She let her help mix potions and revealed to her the secret formula for growing beautiful flowers and delicious vegetables. The only thing she did not allow Rapunzel to do was stray from the house. She was so afraid of losing her that she wouldn't let her to talk to anyone.

Although Rapunzel lived alone with the old witch, it did not stop her from becoming a happy and cheerful child. The little girl loved living in the forest, and she grew into a beautiful young lady. Her long hair kept growing, too. The only thing she ever wanted was to see what lay beyond the trees that surrounded the house. Not a day passed when she did not ask her grandmother to let her go. Every day, she offered to pick the plants that the old woman used for her potions.

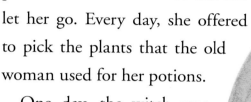

One day, the witch was very impressed with a magic potion that the girl had prepared. Feeling generous, she granted her permission to leave the garden to collect the mushrooms that grew next to a stream.

Rapunzel did not need to be told twice. She clapped with glee, then grabbed a basket. For the first time, Rapunzel left the garden she had lived in for years.

After running to the stream, she stood and looked around in amazement. It was a part of the forest she had never seen before. How many wonderful things there were to be found, just a few minutes' walk from the house!

Rapunzel was so engrossed that she did not notice a knight on his horse, approaching at a gallop. It was only when she heard his laughter that she looked up. Startled, she ran to hide behind a bush. There, she peeked out to see who it was. Through the leaves, she saw a young man jump down from his horse. He tied the horse to a tree, then sat down to wait for his fellow knights, who had fallen behind.

"You are getting to be slow!" laughed the young man when the others caught up with him.

"Really, Your Highness? We'll soon see. Draw your sword, so we can start training!" said the oldest of the group.

For hours the young prince and the other knights pretended to duel in the clearing. A few feet away, Rapunzel watched from her hiding place in fascination.

When she finally saw them move away, the girl got up and started singing to herself.

"I wonder who that boy is?" she said aloud. "They called him 'Your Highness,' but I don't think he is a prince. He is too short!"

"You think I'm short?" said a voice behind her. The prince had returned to the clearing where he had forgotten his sword. But it had completely slipped his mind when he heard the girl's beautiful singing.

"Don't be afraid," he said, approaching slowly. "I just want to know who you are and what your name is."

Hearing the gentle tone of his voice, Rapunzel stopped and turned. She looked the prince in the eye and knew he would not do her any harm.

"My name is Rapunzel," she said with a smile. "And in fact I *do* find you a little too short to be a prince."

The two of them burst out laughing, then continued to talk and joke until sunset. When she saw that it was getting dark, Rapunzel realized that she was terribly late. She had told her grandmother that she would be back for lunch, hours before! She quickly said good-bye to the prince and promised that they would meet again the next day. Then she ran home, clutching the basket of mushrooms.

She had almost reached home when she came across her grandmother, who was out looking for her.

"Rapunzel!" said the witch with relief. "I was very worried! I was afraid that something had happened to you."

"I'm sorry, Grandma. I'm late, I know, but I was having such fun. I laughed so much! Here, I brought you the mushrooms," said the girl, showing her the full basket.

"You laughed so much? Picking mushrooms?" asked the witch.

"No, I enjoyed myself after that—when I met the prince!"

Rapunzel could not have imagined how much those simple words would anger the witch. She took the girl by the shoulders and shook her.

"You met someone and talked to him? He knows where you live?"

"No, Grandma! He doesn't know where our house is. I didn't mean to upset you."

But the witch wouldn't listen. Enraged, she took one of the mushrooms from the basket and whispered a spell.

The mushroom began to grow and expand. It grew taller than the surrounding trees. Rapunzel looked on in terror. With a final movement of her stick, the witch transformed the giant mushroom into a tower. She ordered Rapunzel to enter the tower and climb the stairs to the top. The witch followed her up.

When they had climbed the last step, the witch made the stairs disappear and removed the door. The only way out of the tower was a small window. Rapunzel stuck her head out of the window and looked down below.

"Grandma," she said. "This tower is really high! And there's no door. How do we get out?"

"This is not a problem that concerns you, Rapunzel. From now on, this tower is your home. You will never leave it!"

Rapunzel burst into tears. She apologized over and over, but the witch was unmoved. She had almost lost the girl forever and was never going to give her the chance to meet anyone else. She then threw Rapunzel's long hair out of the window, and used it as a rope to climb down from the tower.

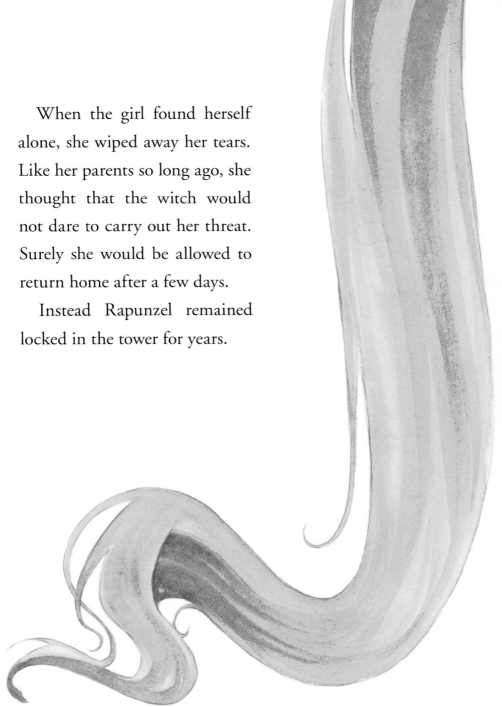

When the girl found herself alone, she wiped away her tears. Like her parents so long ago, she thought that the witch would not dare to carry out her threat. Surely she would be allowed to return home after a few days.

Instead Rapunzel remained locked in the tower for years.

And for years the prince continued to look for her. The day after their meeting he returned to the stream, hoping to see her again. Although he did not find her, he returned the next day, and the next. He continued to return to the forest until snow covered the clearing where they had first met. It was then that the king asked him to forget the girl that no one but the prince had ever seen.

"You said she had a beautiful voice, long blond hair, and that she seemed to have disappeared into thin air," said the king to his son. "Perhaps it was a forest fairy, who bewitched you with her smile. I want you to stop thinking about her. Go traveling for a few years. Seeing the world that lies beyond our borders can only do you good."

So the prince began a long journey that kept him away for years. But he never forgot the girl. When he finally returned to the palace, the first thing he did was take his horse and gallop into the forest. He had almost reached the stream when he heard a song he recognized immediately.

The prince stopped his horse and followed the voice through the forest. This led him to a very high tower, hidden among the trees by a thick spiny hedge that had grown around it. At the top of the tower, a girl was singing at a small window. It was the beautiful girl he had been trying to find for so many years.

He immediately went around the tower to find the door. But there was no opening in the wall of the tower, and it was impossible to get through the spiny bush.

He wondered how he could get Rapunzel out of that strange house. Then he realized with horror that it was actually a prison. The young woman was locked up in the tower! She could not get out, and no one could enter. He wondered who could do something so cruel. Then he heard someone approaching and hurried to hide.

From behind a tree, he saw an old woman. When she reached the foot of the tower, she clapped her hands and shouted:

"Rapunzel, Rapunzel,
let down your hair!"

When Rapunzel heard the witch, she gathered up her
long blond hair, which had never been cut. Then she let
it tumble out the window, as she had done many times in
the past. The witch grabbed hold of it, climbed up to the
window, and went in.

The prince remained hidden until he saw the witch
climb down from the tower and leave. He waited a few
hours to be safe, then he walked over to the tower.

"Rapunzel, Rapunzel, let down your
hair," he cried.

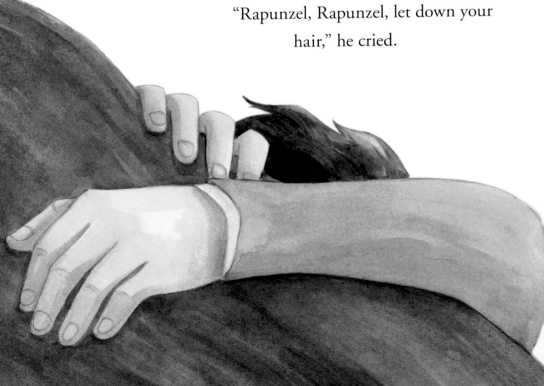

Hearing these words, the girl was very surprised and looked out to see who had called to her. But night had fallen and the forest was too dark. Rapunzel let her hair down and waited to see who would appear. When the prince came through the window, the girl was very frightened and hid in a closet.

"Rapunzel, it is me. Do not be afraid!" said the prince. Then he remembered a detail and added, "I know I've grown taller since the last time we met. Maybe now I look more like a prince to you?"

Astonished, Rapunzel came out of her hiding place. She looked in the stranger's eyes and suddenly recognized that kind look. It was the same one she saw in her dreams every night.

"It's you! I can't believe it, you're here!" she said.

Rapunzel ran over and embraced him.

"I looked for you everywhere," the prince whispered. "I waited for you every day for months!"

"I was locked up here!" said Rapunzel. She began to explain who the old woman he had seen really was. "In recent years I have discovered everything. Not only did she deceive me, but she also stole me from my real parents. She locked me up here, fearing that I might leave her."

"I'll get you out of here," promised the prince. "I'll take you away to the other side of the world so she cannot find you."

The two of them spent the whole night talking. He told her of his travels and adventures; she spoke of her dreams and hopes.

"You'd better go now," Rapunzel said when she saw the first rays of sun coming in the window. "The witch might come, and I dread to think of what she could do to you."

"I'll be back tonight, so we can make a plan to escape and marry!"

He slid down the tower using her long hair and stopped in the clearing to blow her a kiss.

Unfortunately, the witch had just emerged from the forest and saw him. Furious, she waited for the prince to go away. Then she walked over to the tower and asked Rapunzel to let her up.

As soon as she went in through the window, she noticed that something had happened: the girl singing merrily as she tidied the room was very different from the sad and silent girl she was used to. The witch decided to act immediately. Rapunzel would always be hers and no one else's!

She raised her stick and softly whispered a spell. Rapunzel immediately fell to the ground, asleep. Picking up a large pair of scissors, the witch approached the girl and cut off her long hair. She then tightly tied the hair to the window.

With a second spell she created a long spiral staircase that led out of the tower. The old witch picked up the sleeping girl and slowly carried her down the stairs. She carried her all the way to a nearby cave in the forest. There, she placed Rapunzel down and went back out. With more magic words, she dragged a large stone across the entrance of the cave. Rapunzel was trapped inside.

The witch looked with satisfaction at the new prison she had created for Rapunzel. Then she quickly returned to the tower, climbed the steps, and waited for the prince.

At sunset, he reached the tower and called out to Rapunzel to help him climb up. The witch threw down the hair she had cut and prepared to welcome him.

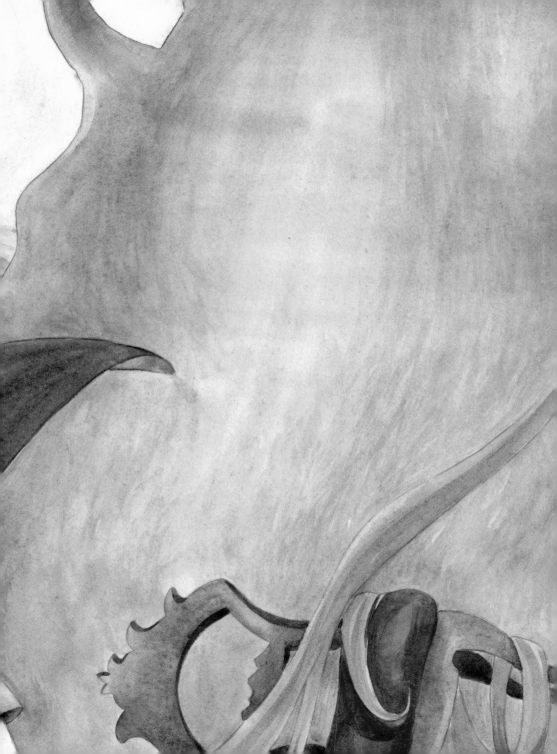

When the prince reached the window, he saw that the hair he had used to climb the tower was tied to the window.

"Rapunzel? Rapunzel!" he called out in fear.

"She's not here and she can't hear you," said a voice behind him. The prince turned and came face to face with the witch.

"Where is she?"

"Near here, in fact. She's locked up in a cave in the forest, but you will not find her."

"What spell did you cast on her, evil creature?"

"She's just sleeping. I would never hurt her," the witch replied. "But that is not true for you!"

The witch pointed her stick at him and out shot a spark. The prince jumped back and was only grazed lightly by the cursed spark. But in doing so he fell from the tower and into the spiny hedge. He was still alive, but when he opened his eyes he was horrified to discover that he was blinded by the curse. As he tried to get up, he heard the witch scream:

"Now you'll never
find Rapunzel!"

When Rapunzel awoke, she was devastated to find herself in a new prison. She tried to move the stone that sealed the cave, but it would not budge. Just when it seemed that all hope was lost, she remembered that her voice had led the young man to her. So she started to sing.

The prince was in the forest, and could see nothing. With each step he stumbled and fell to the ground, but he refused to give up. He had to find Rapunzel. After several hours he thought he heard her voice. Exhausted, he finally arrived at the mouth of the cave. Together, they managed to move the stone. Rapunzel, finally free, flew to the prince's arms.

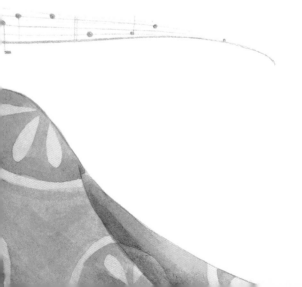

When she saw what the witch had done to him, she clutched him and began to cry. But as her pure tears fell on the young man's face, they broke the curse and restored the prince's sight. Rapunzel immediately stopped crying and hugged the prince. He picked her up and twirled her round until they both fell to the ground, laughing.

"We're still not safe," said the prince, becoming serious. "We have to take my horse and go far away from here. Come with me."

Taking Rapunzel by the hand, the prince returned to his horse near the tower. They did not know that the witch was up in the tower, watching them. She picked up her stick, and pointed it down at the thorny bush. But as she leaned out, she lost her balance! Screaming, she fell and landed on the thorns, which had been awakened by her magic. They grabbed hold of the witch and squeezed her until she suffocated.

Rapunzel looked away in horror. When she finally opened her eyes, she took a deep breath and sighed. "Now I am really free. Take me away from here."

The prince helped her onto his horse, and together they rode off. At sunset they arrived at the gates of a grand palace. The prince took Rapunzel into the throne room and presented her to the king and queen as his future bride.

"Welcome, my dear," said the queen. "We have heard a lot about you."

"Tomorrow the preparations for the wedding will begin," added the king. "But now you must be tired. I will prepare for you the most beautiful room at the top of the tower."

"NO!" shouted the prince and Rapunzel at the same time.

"No towers, Father. We've had enough of towers," said the prince with a laugh.

The following weeks were filled with excitement for Rapunzel. Gradually the young woman became accustomed to life at court. Lavish banquets were held in her honor, at which she participated as the future king's betrothed.

One afternoon, Rapunzel seemed distracted.

"You look sad," remarked the prince. "What's the matter?"

"I was thinking about my parents. I haven't seen them for so long. For years I even thought they were dead. But since I realized that this was just another of the witch's lies, I have been wondering where they are. I wish I could see them. I know it is impossible . . ."

"Maybe it's not impossible. I will send my best knights to every corner of the kingdom. They will visit every village and town. I'm sure that we will find them."

At sunset, ten of the most trusted knights in the kingdom set out. Each took with him a scroll of parchment sealed with wax, containing a message from the young woman to her parents. Every morning for over a month, Rapunzel awoke full of hope. But none of the knights ever returned.

Finally, the day of the wedding came. The young woman opened her eyes, thinking that she had never felt so happy. If only her parents could have been there, then everything would be perfect. Suddenly the prince knocked on the door.

"Open up, Rapunzel, I have a surprise!"

"You cannot see the bride before the wedding. It's bad luck!" she laughed.

"Okay, I'll close my eyes, even if I will miss your smile when you see your parents."

Rapunzel ran to open the door and saw Nicholas and Anna. They smiled at her, their eyes shining. She hugged her parents and everything was perfect.

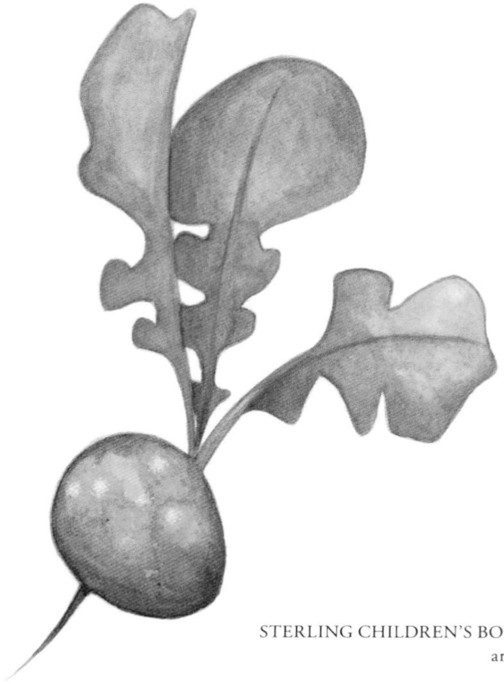

STERLING CHILDREN'S BOOKS
New York

An Imprint of Sterling Publishing
387 Park Avenue South
New York, NY 10016

First Sterling edition 2015
First published in Italy in 2014 by De Agostini Libri S.p.A.

ISBN 978-1-4549-1511-9

Distributed in Canada by Sterling Publishing
c/o Canadian Manda Group, 165 Dufferin Street
Toronto, Ontario, Canada M6K 3H6
For information about custom editions, special sales, and premium and corporate purchases,
please contact Sterling Special Sales at 800-805-5489 or specialsales@sterlingpublishing.com.

Translation: Contextus s.r.l., Pavia, Italy (Louise Bostock)
Editor: Contextus s.r.l., Pavia, Italy (Martin Maguire)

Manufactured in China
Lot #:
2 4 6 8 10 9 7 5 3 1
11/14
www.sterlingpublishing.com/kids